SIMON SPOTLIGHT
An imprint of Simon & Schuster Children's Publishing Division
1230 Avenue of the Americas, New York, New York 10020
This Simon Spotlight edition September 2022
Copyright © 2022 by Simon & Schuster, Inc. All rights reserved, including the right of reproduction in whole or in part in any form.
SIMON SPOTLIGHT and colophon are registered trademarks of Simon & Schuster, Inc.
YOU'RE INVITED TO A CREEPOVER is a registered trademark of Simon & Schuster, Inc. For information about special discounts for bulk purchases, please contact Simon & Schuster Special Sales at 1-866-506-1949 or business@simonandschuster.com.
Designed by Nicholas Sciacca. Text by Matthew J. Gilbert. Based on the text by Ellie O'Ryan. Art Services by Glass House Graphics. Pencils & Inks by Onofrio Orlando. Colors by Giusi Lo Piccolo, Color Assistants Nataliya Torretta, Francesca Ingrassia and Santino Triolo. Lettering by Giuseppe Naselli/Grafimated Cartoon. Supervision by Salvatore Di Marco/Grafimated Cartoon. The illustrations for this book were rendered digitally.
Manufactured in China 0522 SCP
10 9 8 7 6 5 4 3 2 1
ISBN 978-1-6659-1564-9 (hc)
ISBN 978-1-6659-1563-2 (pbk)
ISBN 978-1-6659-1565-6 (ebook)
Library of Congress Catalog Card Number 2022934417

TRUTH OR DARE...

WRITTEN BY P. J. NIGHT
ILLUSTRATED BY ONOFRIO ORLANDO
AT GLASS HOUSE GRAPHICS

SIMON SPOTLIGHT
NEW YORK   LONDON   TORONTO   SYDNEY   NEW DELHI

CHAPTER 1

9

OH? DOING WHAT?

CAN'T TELL YOU. NO *GIRLS* ALLOWED.

KIDDING! I'M GOING TO A MOVIE WITH JAKE AND TOBY.

OBVIOUSLY, SNACKS WERE OUR TOP PRIORITY.

NICE! TELL JAKE I SAID HI. WE GOTTA GO!

SEE YOU LATER, MAX.

WOW! DID YOU SEE THAT?

HE GAVE ME A CANDY BAR!

I MEAN... KIND OF...

YOU STILL HAVE TO PAY FOR IT.

THUNK

HE IS SO CUTE! I WISH I DIDN'T GET SO TONGUE-TIED AROUND HIM.

WHO'S UP FOR A LITTLE... *TRUTH OR DARE?*

SOUNDS FUN! HOW ABOUT THE PERSON WITH THE MOST MAKEUP GOES FIRST?

HAHAHAHA?

THAT MEANS... LEAH!

THIS MAYBE-TOO-MUCH-MAKEUP IS ALL ABBY'S DOING, SO I THINK SHE SHOULD GO FIRST.

I'LL GO, I'M NOT SCARED.

ABBY WONDERED IF EVERYONE ELSE WAS THINKING ABOUT WHAT HAPPENED...

...THE TRAGEDY, LAST YEAR...

UMMM... LEAH, WHAT ARE YOU DOING?

NOT MUCH... JUST THOUGHT I'D TEXT JAKE TO SAY HI...

NOOOOO!!!

IT'S LIKE YOU TOLD ME...

HOW WILL YOU EVER GET THE CHANCE TO GO OUT WITH HIM IF YOU DON'T TALK TO HIM?

I'M JUST TRYING TO HELP.

FINE, JUST LET ME DO IT. I'LL DO IT.

ABBY'S THOUGHTS WERE GOING A MILE A MINUTE...

JAKE AND I ARE FRIENDS. WE'VE KNOWN EACH OTHER FOREVER...

IT WOULDN'T BE TOTALLY WEIRD FOR ME TO TEXT HIM. PROBABLY.

HOME
JAKE
JENNA
LEAH

WHAT DO I WRITE?

GAAAAHHHHHH!!!!

DING!

WHAT'D HE SAY? IS IT HIM?

"HEY! I'M HANGING OUT WITH MAX AND TOBY. HOW ARE THE MAKEOVERS GOING?"

MAKE-OVERS?

WHAT IS HE-OH...

THEY SAW OUR WILD MAKE-OVERS!

BUT HOW?

JAKE

Hey!

Hey!
I'm hanging out with Max and Toby

How are the makeovers going?

Let's just say I don't think anyone is going to ask me to do their makeup again

But you are an artist!

I have a feeling I'm never going to hear the end of this...

Definitely not

G2g, c u Monday, bye 4 now

...

WAIT, WHY ARE YOU TELLING HIM BYE?

I FIGURED I'D QUIT WHILE I WAS AHEAD.

I'M TURNING IT OFF BEFORE I SAY SOMETHING DUMB.

WHO'S UP FOR A SCARY MOVIE...?

AWESOME, YES!

GOOD, I'M READY TO CLIMB INTO MY SLEEPING BAG.

31

GASP!

BZZZZ!

IT'S... JUST...MY PHONE.

I THOUGHT I HAD TURNED THIS OFF...?

WHAT? WHAT'S WRONG?

UNKNOWN

LEAVE HIM ALONE, HE'S MINE! DON'T MAKE ME TELL YOU TWICE!

WHAT'S IT SAY?

33

I ALWAYS SLEEP NEXT TO MY PHONE.

HOW DID IT GET ALL THE WAY OVER HERE?

DID ONE OF YOU MOVE—?

WE DIDN'T TOUCH YOUR PHONE. WE WERE ALL ASLEEP!

PLUS, YOU'RE, LIKE, THE NICEST GIRL IN THE WORLD. NOBODY HERE WOULD MESS WITH YOU LIKE THAT.

YOU REALLY THINK THIS IS NO BIG DEAL...?

TOTALLY! C'MON, LET'S CALM DOWN AND TRY TO GET SOME SLEEP.

FOR THE FIRST TIME IN A LONG TIME, ABBY DIDN'T WANT TO SLEEP ANYWHERE NEAR HER PHONE.

LUCKILY FOR HER, DAYBREAK CAME SOON ENOUGH. SHE DIDN'T SLEEP A WINK.

WE COULD TEXT JAKE, ASK HIM IF HE OR HIS FRIENDS SENT THAT TEXT. YOU KNOW, AS A PRANK?

THOSE BOYS *DO* LIKE TO PULL PRANKS.

NO! I DON'T WANT ANYONE OUTSIDE OF THE SLEEPOVER TO KNOW WHAT HAPPENED.

BYE! SEE YOU AT SCHOOL!

BYE, ABBY. MESSAGE YOU LATER, OKAY?

OF COURSE!

GET SOME SLEEP! YOU NEED IT.

NEED A NAP? UP LATE HAVING TOO MUCH FUN, HUH?

YEAH, SOMETHING LIKE THAT.

39

ABBY TRIED NOT TO THINK OF THE TEXT MESSAGE. TRIED NOT TO THINK OF *HER*.

SHE SLEPT ALL DAY.

DING!

UNTIL SHE WAS WOKEN UP BY ANOTHER MESSAGE. THIS ONE FROM...

LEAH!

CLICK

LOADING...

Sara James Memorial Scholarship Foundation

GASP!

It's still so sad what happened to her 😟

THE CAR LOST CONTROL. IT SWERVED ONTO THE SIDEWALK—

IT WAS THE WORST TRAGEDY RIVERDALE HAD EVER SUFFERED.

AND EVERYONE REALLY SUFFERED.

ESPECIALLY JAKE.

CHAPTER 4

THE NEXT DAY, AT SCHOOL...

WHAT'S THE HOLD UP? WHAT'S GOING ON?

MAYBE IT'S SOMETHING EXCITING?

EXCITING? HERE? YEAH, RIGHT.

DO YOU WANT TO WALK HOME TOGETHER?

SURE, YEAH.

I'LL COME MEET YOU AT YOUR LOCKER AFTER THE BELL THEN. SEE YA!

BYE.

FIRST DANCE OF THE SCHOOL YEAR

UMMM... YOU KNOW YOU'RE TEXTING ME RIGHT AFTER, RIGHT? LIKE RIGHT AFTER.

OKAY, YES, I PROMISE!

IT USUALLY FELT LIKE TIME CRAWLED TO THE LAST BELL.

BUT TODAY, IT FELT LIKE AN ACTUAL ETERNITY FOR ABBY, UNTIL IT FINALLY—

RIIIIIING!

RIIIIIING!

SO...EXCITED ABOUT SUMMER VACATION?

YEAH, ONLY EIGHT MONTHS LEFT TO GO. IT'LL BE A BREEZE—

UGH, DON'T REMIND ME.

THIS DANCE, HUH? TURNED INTO A BIG DEAL ALL OF A SUDDEN.

I KNOW, RIGHT?! DOESN'T TAKE MUCH TO GET PEOPLE EXCITED IN THIS TOWN.

ARE YOU...?

I MEAN... ARE YOU GOING?

I THINK SO. I DON'T KNOW.

IF YOU DO DECIDE TO GO...DO YOU WANT A RIDE?

MY MOM'S GONNA DRIVE ME, AND I FIGURED, I LIVE ACROSS THE STREET. IT'D BE WEIRD IF I DIDN'T ASK YOU IF YOU NEED A RIDE—

I'D LOVE TO.

WHEW! THAT COULD HAVE BEEN AWKWARD, HAHA.

YEAH, WELL, HERE'S MY HOUSE.

OH, RIGHT! COOL.

SO...SEVEN ON SATURDAY NIGHT SOUND OKAY?

SEVEN ON SATURDAY.

DEEP BREATH

SQUEEEEEEE!

ABBY!

YES, MOM?

CAN YOU PLEASE TAKE CHESTER OUT? I'M ON A WORK CALL, AND I CAN'T HAVE HIM BARKING THROUGH IT.

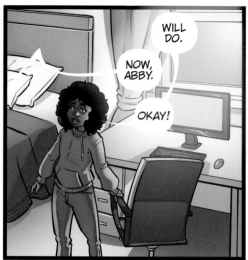

WILL DO.

NOW, ABBY.

OKAY!

CHESTER! TIME FOR A WALK!

CHESTER... HERE, CUTIE! C'MON, COME GET READY FOR WALKIES.

JINGLE JINGLE JINGLE

GRRRRR...

CHESTER, COME! CHESTER...?

WOOF!

CHAPTER 5

WHO'S OUT HERE?

NO ONE.

GOOD JOB, ABBY.

OH, NOW YOU'RE TOTALLY FINE! THANKS A LOT, CHESTER.

WAY TO SCARE A GIRL TO DEATH.

DUSK MEANT IT WAS TIME FOR THEM TO TURN BACK.

AND TIME FOR ABBY TO TURN THIS NIGHT AROUND.

HEY! CHESTER FINALLY CALMED DOWN?

YES.

WAS IT A SQUIRREL?

IT WAS A BIG OL' FALSE ALARM.

CLASSIC CHESTER.

SNIFF

LASAGNA?

YEP. GONNA BE DELICIOUS. READY IN ABOUT A HALF HOUR.

UM, MOM, CAN I ASK YOU SOMETHING?

OF COURSE.

THERE'S A SCHOOL DANCE ON SATURDAY, AND JAKE...

...SORT OF OFFERED ME A RIDE, SO...CAN I GO?

MOM, WHAT? DON'T SMILE LIKE THAT. IT'S JUST A RIDE.

EXCITED FOR YOU! WHAT ARE YOU GONNA WEAR?

WHOOOSH!

AAAHHHH!!!

KIDDO! IT'S ME, DAD!

WHAT ARE YOU EVEN DOING BACK HERE?

I THOUGHT I SAW YOU RUN BACK HERE AS I WAS PULLING INTO THE DRIVEWAY.

I DIDN'T MEAN TO FRIGHTEN YOU.

YOU OKAY?

I'M OKAY. I JUST THOUGHT... I SAW SOMEONE.

THAT'S ALL.

HOW ABOUT WE GO HOME?

YOU SHOULDN'T BE OUT HERE THIS LATE. THERE ARE DANGEROUS THINGS IN THESE WOODS.

THERE ARE DANGEROUS THINGS BACK AT HOME, TOO, SHE WANTED TO SAY.

BUT SHE DIDN'T SAY A WORD.

Hey. What's up?

JUST CAUGHT A GIRL STARING IN MY WINDOW!!!!

WHAT???

I followed her into the woods, but she disappeared

Her hair looked just like...

??

I know it sounds crazy, but her hair looked just like...Sara's

I'm really freaking out

Take a breath. Relax.

Everybody has been talking a lot about Sara w/ the dance and all

And u might just be feeling strange bc you're going on a date

With Jake

I am sure you just imagined it

A FOOTPRINT.

OH... MY...

AND THEN, ANOTHER. AND ANOTHER.

STEP BY STEP, ABBY WALKED ACROSS THE ROOM, HER HANDS STARTING TO SHAKE.

SHE DREADED OPENING THE CLOSET DOOR.

WHO—*OR WHAT*— WOULD SHE FIND BEHIND IT?

JUST DO IT. ONE-TWO- THREE—

CREAAAAAK

CHAPTER 7

SOMETHING CRAZY IS DEF GOING ON! I JUST FOUND MY BRAND-NEW TOP RIPPED UP!!!

HUH?

I RAN OUTSIDE TO FOLLOW THAT GIRL, AND I THREW THE TOP ON MY BED, BUT WHEN I GOT BACK, IT WAS HANGING IN THE CLOSET, TORN TO PIECES!!

LEAH, SOMETHING REALLY SCARY IS GOING ON!

Ok, ok, calm down. There has to be a reasonable explanation for all this

Chester? Could he have chewed it up?

AND THEN HUNG IT UP IN THE CLOSET HIMSELF?

HE'S A DOG

DON'T YELL @ ME! I AM JUST TRYING TO HELP YOU

No offense, but it seems like U are trying to freak URSELF out

??

It's not enough for u that the guy u like asked u to the dance

Now u have to make up drama so u can be the center of attention?

GIVE IT A REST, LEAH.

BEEP.

THIS OUGHT TO BE GOOD.

UNKNOWN

I'M WARNING YOU. STAY AWAY FROM HIM!!!! NEXT TIME I WILL DO SOMETHING MUCH WORSE!

IT'S HER.

ABBY DROPPED HER PHONE, AND IT SLID RIGHT UNDER HER BED.

YEAH... I'M DEFINITELY NOT IMAGINING THIS.

AS ABBY CLIMBED OUT FROM UNDER THE BED...

...THE AIR IN THE ROOM SUDDENLY WENT COLD.

SOMETHING WAS PULLING HER BACK UNDER.

ABBY WANTED TO SCREAM, BUT SHE COULDN'T. HER VOICE CRACKED INTO NOTHING—

...

ABBY COULDN'T ESCAPE.

COULDN'T MOVE.

COULDN'T BREATHE.

GASP!

CHAPTER 8

ABBY!

MOM! HELP! I CAN'T GET OUT!

WOOF! WOOF!

SHHH—CHESTER—SHHH—IT'S OKAY.

GRRRR

KIDDO, WE'RE HERE, CALM DOWN.

YOUR SHIRT IS JUST CAUGHT ON SOMETHING, HONEY—

FEELS LIKE IT'S CAUGHT ON THE BED FRAME. HOLD STILL.

WHEN DID THE POWER COME BACK ON?

WHAT? THE POWER NEVER WENT OFF.

ABBY, ARE YOU FEELING OKAY? WHAT'S GOING ON?

ABBY COULD SEE IT ON THEIR FACES. THEY WOULD NEVER BELIEVE HER ABOUT WHAT *REALLY JUST HAPPENED.*

I COULD SHOW THEM THE TEXTS, SHE THOUGHT. BUT WHAT IF...THEY FREAK AND TAKE MY PHONE AWAY?

IT DIDN'T SEEM WORTH THE RISK.

MY PHONE FELL UNDER THE BED. IT'S NOT IMPORTANT.

FORGET IT.

COME ON. SOME LASAGNA WILL HELP YOU FEEL BETTER.

UMMM... MAYBE WE GIVE THE PHONES A REST AND JUST CHAT LIKE HUMAN BEINGS OVER DINNER. WHADDAYA SAY?

WITH PLEASURE.

WOW, I CAN'T BELIEVE THAT WORKED! YOU HIT YOUR HEAD UNDER THE BED, KIDDO?

FIRST A HUG? THEN WILLINGLY NOT TAKING YOUR PHONE TO THE DINNER TABLE?

THUMP

WHO ARE YOU AND WHAT HAVE YOU DONE WITH MY DAUGHTER?

OH HAHA. VERY FUNNY.

WHEN THE PARANORMAL GETS PERSONAL

"...SPIRITS LONG FOR MORE. MORE TIME WITH LOVED ONES..."

"...OTHER SPIRITS ARE VENGEFUL AND CAN CREATE HAUNTINGS."

"...CURSED IMAGES OF THE DEAD APPEARING IN PHOTOS WITH THE LIVING."

GHOST PROOF!!

Ghost Video

Ghostbusters

Vampire Proof

Exor

Pet G

"...THERE ARE WAYS TO HELP A MISGUIDED SPIRIT FIND ITS WAY TO THE OTHER REALM."

GHOST PROOF!!

The top right is a browser window titled "Séance Suggestions".

Séance Suggestions

"FOR A SÉANCE TO BE TRULY SUCCESSFUL..."

"...IT REQUIRES TWO TO THREE PEOPLE. BELIEVERS."

CLICK

HOW CAN I MAKE YOU BELIEVE ME, LEAH?

TO: Leah601

FROM: AbbyGirl

SUBJECT: Sorry

Hey Leah,

First, I'm sorry I hung up on you. I'm really stressing out. So many weird things have been happening, and some of them you don't even know about. So I'm going to tell you everything. Please hear me out before assuming it's just my imagination. I wish it was. Because then I could control it and make it STOP.

At my sleepover, I got a scary text message in the middle of the night. And my phone was on—not the way I left it when we went to sleep.

Then earlier, I saw a girl who looked like Sara running away from my window! When I got back to my room, my top was not where I left it, and I found it shredded in my closet. All that stuff is VERY weird. Don't you agree?

Then things got even scarier. I got another freaky text message from that same number today. After I read it, my room went icy cold. The phone got sucked under my bed, and when I went to grab it, I felt like something was pulling me under. I was terrified. If just one or two of these things happened, I would think it was a coincidence. Or maybe even my imagination. But all this together…I mean, how could I imagine those texts? Or my top getting ripped up? These things are completely real, and you can come see them for your-self if you don't believe me.

I need to make this stop NOW, and I have an idea. But I need your help.

Can you meet me at school tomorrow morning before class starts? 8 a.m.? You are my best friend, Leah. Please help.

<3

Abby

SEND 📎 ∨ □ Tt B I **A** ☰ ☰ ☰ ◇ ☺ ᴬᴮᶜ✓ ✓

97

CHAPTER 9

THE NEXT MORNING...

OKAY, CHESTER, OKAY, ENOUGH, I'M UP—

NEW MESSAGE

Leah601

To: AbbyGirl
From: Leah601
RE: Sorry

Abby,
Everything is fine.
Meet u @ the flagpole

L.

DAAAAAD!
CAN I GET A
RIDE TO—

RIVERDALE
MIDDLE SCHOOL

WHERE
ARE YOU,
LEAH?

SO, WHAT DO YOU—

DID I DO SOMETHING—

YOU GO FIRST.

DID I DO SOMETHING TO UPSET YOU? WHY DID YOU GET SO MAD AT ME OVER TEXT?

IT'S NOT IMPORTANT— IT WAS DUMB, OKAY? I BLEW UP AT YOU, AND I DON'T KNOW WHY.

LOOK, IT'S NOT THAT I DON'T BELIEVE YOU, BUT I DON'T BELIEVE...*IN GHOSTS.*

DEAD IS DEAD. SARA IS DEAD. THAT'S IT.

I KNOW SHE'S DEAD, BUT LOOK AT THIS.

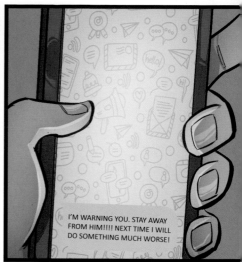
I'M WARNING YOU. STAY AWAY FROM HIM!!!! NEXT TIME I WILL DO SOMETHING MUCH WORSE!

YOU THINK THE "HIM" IS JAKE?

HE'S THE ONLY "HIM" I'M INTO. IT'S GOTTA BE HIM.

AND THAT MEANS THIS MESSAGE IS FROM *HER*.

ABBY, I'M NOT TRYING TO BE MEAN HERE, BUT...

I DON'T KNOW MANY GHOSTS WITH CELLPHONE PLANS.

LEAH, THIS IS SERIOUS!

I CAN TELL YOU'RE UPSET, AND I WANT TO HELP YOU, BELIEVE ME—

CHAPTER 10

THAT EVENING, ABBY PUT HER PLAN INTO MOTION...

...A SÉANCE ...FOR SARA.

IS THIS SOME KIND OF *SHRINE*?

ACCORDING TO SOME RESEARCH I DID ONLINE, YOU NEED AN IMAGE OF THE DECEASED FOR A SÉANCE TO WORK.

THAT AND—

AND...?

YOU NEED AT LEAST TWO PEOPLE...WHO ARE READY TO *BELIEVE*.

I NEED TO KNOW BEFORE WE START... CAN YOU TAKE THIS SERIOUSLY?

IF IT HELPS SARA'S SPIRIT MOVE ON, AND IT HELPS YOU...

...THEN I'M WILLING TO TRY.

SARA, I KNOW YOU'VE BEEN REACHING OUT TO ME, AND I WANT YOU TO KNOW SOMETHING...

...YOU WILL NEVER BE FORGOTTEN. NOT BY YOUR FAMILY, NOT BY YOUR FRIENDS.

AND NOT BY JAKE.

I GET WHY YOU'RE ANGRY. IT'S NOT FAIR WHAT HAPPENED TO YOU—

TAP

TAP

TAP

AND MAYBE YOU FEEL IT'S NOT FAIR FOR JAKE TO TAKE ME TO THE DANCE AND NOT YOU...

114

WE NEED TO MAKE YOUR ROOM LESS CREEPY.

UMMM, LEAH...

MAYBE WE CAN WATCH A MAKEUP TUTORIAL OR—

COME SEE THIS.

PRESENT FOR JAKE IN YOUR TOP DRESSER DRAWER. XOXO, SARA

ABBY, DON'T—

WHAT IF THERE REALLY IS SOMETHING IN THERE—?

I HOPE THERE IS. MAYBE THEN WE CAN ALL FINALLY MOVE ON.

I HAVE A BAD FEELING ABOUT THIS.

YOU WOULDN'T HURT ME, WOULD YOU, SARA?

BREATH

WOW. I NEVER KNEW SARA COULD BE SO MEAN.

ABBY–?

CHAPTER 11

YOU HAVEN'T STARTED COLLECTING OTHER PEOPLE'S HAIR, HAVE YOU?

THIS ISN'T FUNNY, LEAH.

SORRY.

YOU NEED A TOTALLY SUPPORTIVE FRIEND RIGHT NOW...

...AND I'M JUST FINDING ALL THIS A LITTLE HARD TO BELIEVE.

SARA'S SPIRIT HAS BEEN HERE. IT STARTED THE NIGHT OF MY SLEEPOVER WHEN SHE MOVED MY PHONE...

LEAH, WHAT'S WRONG?

I'M GOING TO GO TO THE DANCE WITH JAKE.

NO GHOST IS GOING TO KEEP ME FROM LIVING.

GO, ABBY! YOU'RE SO BRAVE.

FWHOOOSH!

EDNESDAY	THURSDAY	FRIDAY	SATURDAY	SUNDA
X	X	X	X	X
EDNESDAY	THURSDAY	FRIDAY	SATURDAY	SUND
X	X		THE DANCE!!	
EDNESDAY	THURSDAY	FRIDAY	SATURDAY	SUND
EDNESDAY	THURSDAY	FRIDAY	SATURDAY	SUND

THE NEXT DAY, ABBY DECIDED TO PUT THE WHOLE THING TO REST.

SHE REMOVED ALL TRACES OF SARA FROM HER ROOM...

...AND TOOK HER LIFE BACK WITH THE TOUCH OF A BUTTON.

DELETE ALL MESSAGES?

YES

SATURDAY THE DANCE!!

SATURDAY HAD FINALLY ARRIVED.

MOM, I HEARD A CAR. CAN YOU PLEASE GO OUT THERE SO DAD DOESN'T GIVE HIM "THE SPEECH"?

132

CHAPTER 12

ABBY!

I'M GOING HOME.

WAIT, PLEASE... I HAVE TO KNOW...

WHAT DID YOU MEAN WHEN YOU SAID SARA IS WATCHING ME?

I THOUGHT IT WAS OVER, BUT SHE'S STILL HERE. SARA'S SPIRIT IS HERE.

HER SPIRIT HASN'T MOVED ON. SHE'S STILL IN LOVE WITH YOU, JAKE.

SARA HAS BEEN HAUNTING ME AND MESSING WITH ME, SINCE YOU AND I STARTED TALKING.

SHE'S LEFT ME THREATENING TEXTS AND HURTFUL NOTES.

WELL, THAT DOESN'T SOUND LIKE THE SARA I KNEW. AT ALL.

137

AT THE AIRPORT, I COULD TELL EVERYTHING HAD GONE WRONG ALREADY.

AUNT STACY BURST INTO TEARS THE MOMENT SHE SAW ME.

BECAUSE YOU LOOK SO MUCH LIKE SARA?

YES.

I WAS SUPPOSED TO GO TO SCHOOL FOR A SEMES-TER HERE.

BUT UNCLE STEVEN SAID IT WOULD UPSET THE STUDENTS TOO MUCH TO SEE ME.

THEY SAID I'D HAVE TO BE HOMESCHOOLED, THAT I COULDN'T EVEN LEAVE THE HOUSE...

I FELT LIKE A PRISONER, WITH NOWHERE TO GO, AND NO ONE TO TALK TO.

YOU'RE RIGHT. I GUESS I WANTED TO PROVE TO MYSELF THAT... I'M NOT HER.

I DON'T WANT SARA'S LIFE ANYMORE.

I WISH I COULD GO BACK AND UNDO ALL THIS.

I WENT TOO FAR, AND I'M SORRY. I'M JUST SO LONELY.

I FORGIVE YOU.

WHAT—?!

YOU DO?

IT'S WHAT SARA WOULD WANT. YOU SAID SO YOURSELF, JAKE, SHE HAD A BIG HEART.

I THINK SHE WOULD WANT US TO FORGIVE YOU.

WHAT DO YOU SAY, JAKE?

FINE. FORGIVEN.

WOULD YOU LIKE TO HANG OUT SOMETIME, SAMANTHA?

I MIGHT HAVE A SLEEPOVER NEXT WEEKEND, AND I'D LIKE YOU TO COME.

I THINK WE NEED TO GET YOU OUT OF THAT HOUSE. IF YOU WANT.

REALLY?

SURE. WHY NOT. AFTER ALL, YOU ALREADY KNOW WHERE I LIVE.

HAHAHA! HAHA

EPILOGUE

ONE WEEK LATER... AS THE CLOCK STRIKES MIDNIGHT...

OKAY, SAMANTHA, TRUTH OR DARE...?

TRUTH.

WHERE DID YOU CUT YOUR HAIR? IT LOOKS SO STRAIGHT AND EVEN.

YEAH, YOU CAN'T EVEN TELL YOU CUT SOME OF IT OFF.

CUT MY HAIR? WHAT ARE YOU TALKING ABOUT?

149

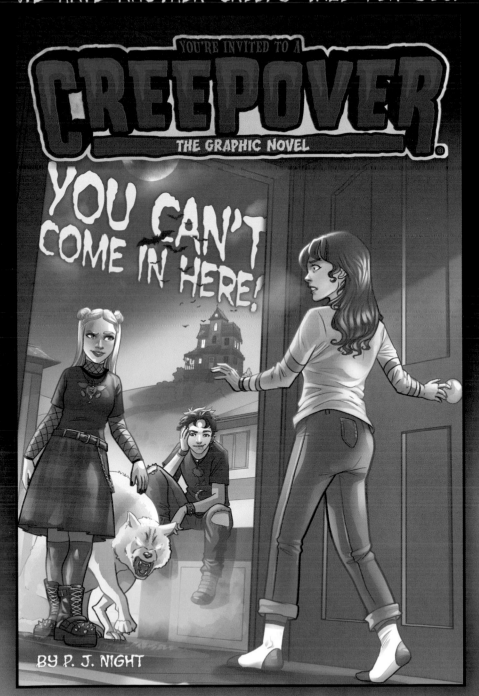

YOU'RE INVITED TO A

CREEPOVER

THE GRAPHIC NOVEL

YOU CAN'T COME IN HERE!

BY P. J. NIGHT